SHOO, FLY GUY!

Tedd Arnold

Cartwheel
·B·O·O·K·S·®

SCHOLASTIC INC.
New York   Toronto   London   Auckland
Sydney   Mexico City   New Delhi   Hong Kong

Specially for Zachary Chase
—T. A.

Library of Congress Cataloging-in-Publication Data:
Arnold, Tedd.
Shoo, Fly Guy! / Tedd Arnold.
p. cm.
"Cartwheel books."
Summary: A pet fly searches for his favorite brown, oozy, lumpy, smelly food.
ISBN 978-0-439-63905-7
[1. Flies—Fiction.] I. Title.
PZ7.A7379Sh 2006
[E]--dc22   2005028746
ISBN 978-0-439-63905-7

39 38 37 36 35   21 22 23 24 25
Printed in China 38
First printing, September 2006

<u>Chapter 1</u>

A boy had a pet fly.
The boy called his pet Fly Guy.
Fly Guy could say the boy's
name—

BUZZ!

Buzz played with Fly Guy.

Buzz made him a glass house.

Best of all, Buzz fed him.

Fly Guy's favorite food
was brown, oozy,
lumpy, and smelly.

One day Fly Guy went
flying by himself.

When he came home,
Buzz was gone.

Dear Fly Guy,
Where are you?
We are going
on a picnic.
We will be
back soon.
Love,
Buzz

Fly Guy was hungry.
So off he flew.

Chapter 2

Fly Guy flew until he
saw something to eat.

It wasn't oozy, lumpy, or smelly. But it was brown. Close enough!

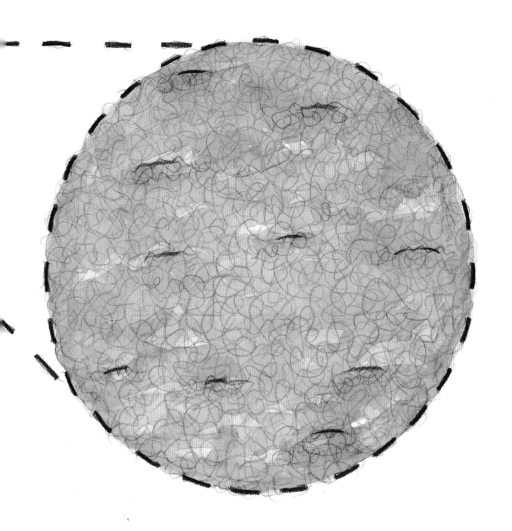

A boy shouted,
"That is my hamburger!"

"Shoo, fly!"

Fly Guy flew on until he
saw something else.

It wasn't brown, lumpy, or smelly. But it was oozy. Close enough!

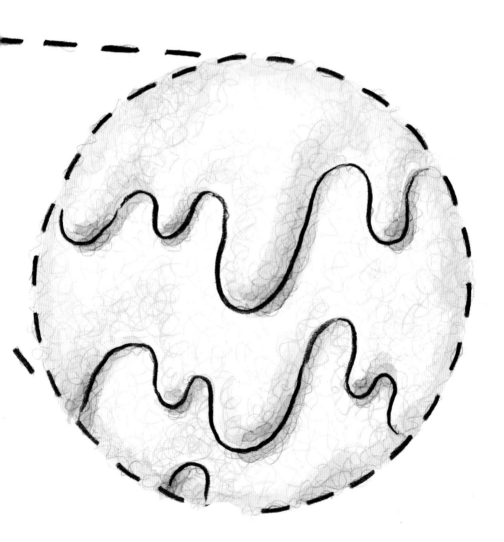

A girl yelled,
"That is my pizza!"

"Shoo, fly!"

Fly Guy flew on until
he saw something else.

It wasn't brown, oozy, or smelly. But it was lumpy. Close enough!

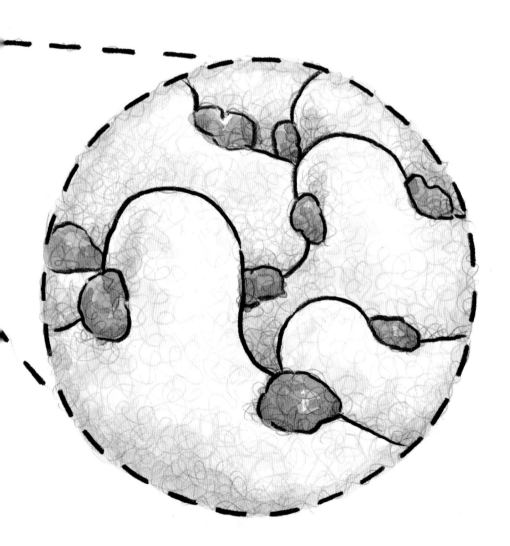

A dog growled,
"Those are my bones."

"Shoo, fly!"

Fly Guy flew on until he
saw something else.

It wasn't brown, oozy, or lumpy. But it was smelly. Close enough!

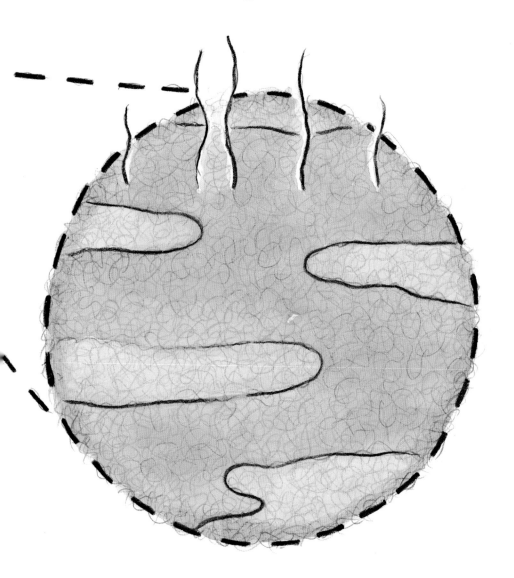

A bird squawked,
"That is my roadkill."

"Shoo, fly!"

Chapter 3

Fly Guy was very hungry.
And he was very tired.
He looked around.
Fly Guy was very lost.

He flew on and on and on and

and on until...

Fly Guy saw something.
Could it be? Yes!

It was brown, oozy,
lumpy, and smelly.

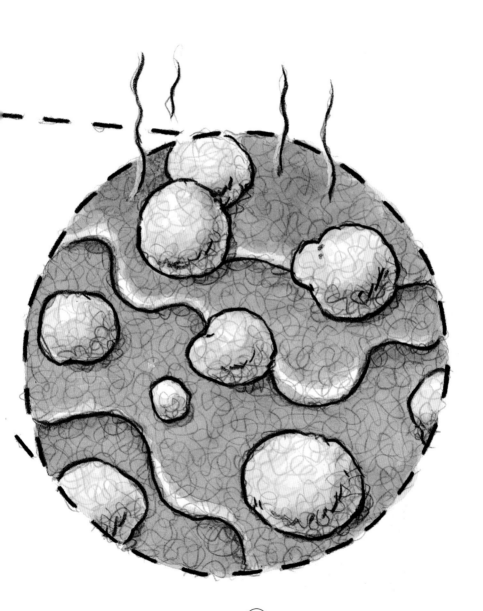

"You found our picnic!"
cried Buzz. "And here is
your favorite—Shoo Fly Pie!"
Fly Guy was very happy!